Why Am I Here?

Constance Ørbeck-Nilssen & Akin Duzakin

Eerdmans Books for Young Readers

Grand Rapids, Michigan

I wonder why I am here,
in this exact place.

What if I were somewhere else —

somewhere completely different from here?

Maybe some place on the other side of the earth.

There are lots of people living there too —

even more than here.

Would I have been someone else, then?

Someone who also wondered "Why am I here?"

What if I lived in a city with millions of people?

All alone.

There are lots of children who do that — live alone.

On the street or under a bridge.

Then I would dream about being somewhere else.

What if there were a war going on where I lived,
and I had to hide until it was safe to come out?
Until the fighting was over.
But what if the war never ended?
Where would I go then?

What if I had to make my way with thousands of others
to an unfamiliar place?
Where no one knew how long we could stay.
Or how long we would have to wait
before going home again.

What if I had to move from place to place?

And the only things I could keep

were what I was able to carry with me.

What would it be like to live like that?

What if I lived in a place

where I had to work all day long,

deep inside a mountain,

where the sunlight doesn't reach.

Even though I was a child.

There are lots of children who have to work.

Could I do it?

What if I lived where there was only desert?

Where the wind formed mountains of sand

and blew away every trace of what had once been there.

Could I live like that?

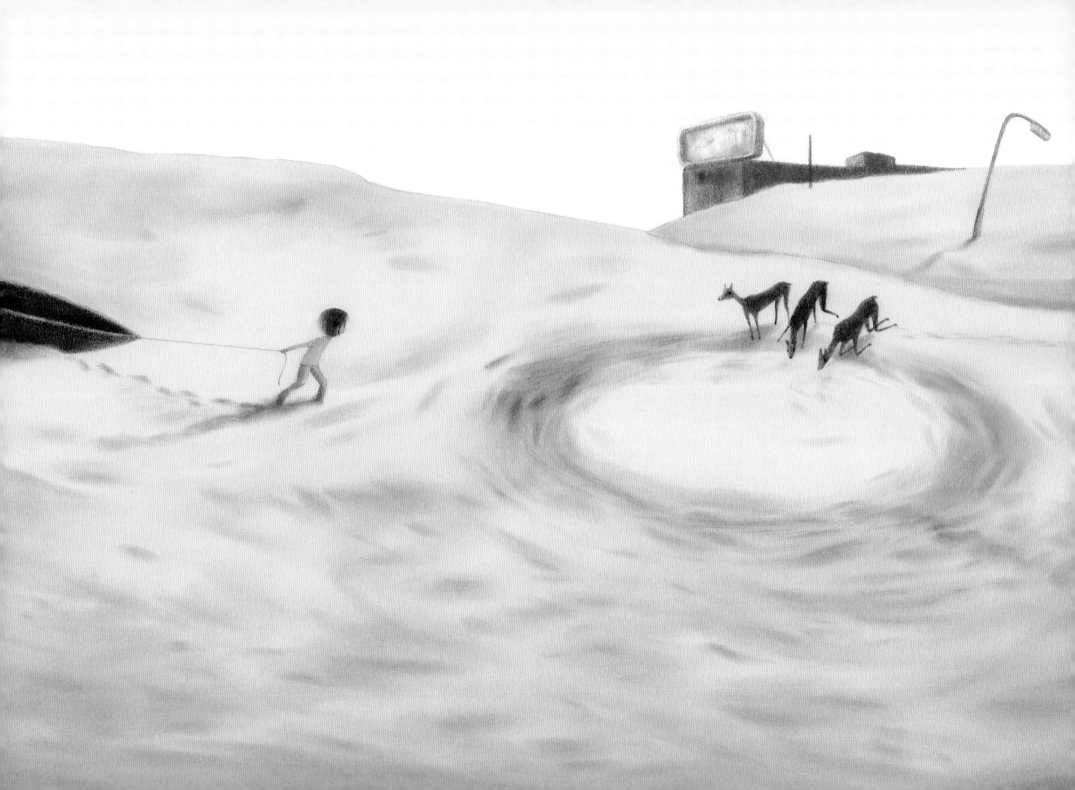

What if I were in a place where there was only ocean
and glaciers and melting icebergs?
Where the northern lights carved a path through the sky
that no one could follow.
What would I do there?

What if I were in a place that no one else knew about?

Somewhere without any roads.

Only deep forests, with rivers that glimmered

like trails through the trees.

And it was so quiet that everything seemed to be holding its breath.

Maybe I wouldn't even know that other places existed.

What if there were floods where I was,

and earthquakes?

And everything was destroyed and wiped away.

And no one had any food or water.

Where would I go then?

Would I come here?

In that case, it would be good if someone said that

I could stay here.

Because this is where I should be.

Isn't that just the way it is?

This is the only place I know.

I was born here, and all the people I love live here too.

Maybe one day I will move somewhere else.

I wonder if there is anyone who knows why we're here.

Or do we just think we know?

Maybe there are other people who wonder the same thing.

What if I were just here, without thinking about it?

Everything might have been different
if I were somewhere else.
Why am I me, and not someone else?
And why am I here?

Maybe that's how it is —
I am my own house.
And I will be at home
wherever I am.

Constance Ørbeck-Nilssen studied at the Norwegian Journalist Academy in Oslo and completed the writing program at the Norwegian Institute for Children's Books. She now works as a freelance journalist and children's author, and she has written a number of picture books. She lives in Norway.

Akin Duzakin is a Turkish-Norwegian illustrator and children's author. In 2006 he won the Bokkunstprisen award for illustration, and he was nominated for the Astrid Lindgren Memorial Award in 2007 and 2008. He and Constance Ørbeck-Nilssen have also collaborated on *I'm Right Here* (Eerdmans). Akin lives in Norway. Visit his website at www.akinduzakin.com.

First published in the United States in 2016 by
Eerdmans Books for Young Readers, an imprint of Wm. B. Eerdmans Publishing Co.
2140 Oak Industrial Dr. NE • Grand Rapids, Michigan 49505 • www.eerdmans.com/youngreaders

Originally published in Norway in 2014 under the title *Hvorfor er jeg her?*
by Magikon forlag, Kolbotn, Norway • www.magikon.no
Text by Constance Ørbeck-Nilssen • Illustrations by Akin Duzakin
© 2014 Magikon forlag • Translated from the original Norwegian into English by Becky Crook
English language translation provided by Magikon forlag and edited by Eerdmans Books for Young Readers

Manufactured at Tien Wah Press in Malaysia

21 20 19 18 17 16   1 2 3 4 5 6 7 8 9

ISBN 978-0-8028-5477-3

A catalog record of this book is available from the Library of Congress

Illustrations created with pastels and colored pencils on paper • Text type set in Baskerville

This translation is published with the support of NORLA, Norwegian Literature Abroad.